W9-ANN-402

Here are some other Holt books you will enjoy:

FROZEN GIRL
by David Getz

FROZEN MAN
by David Getz

LIFE ON MARS
by David Getz

MUMMY MYSTERIES
by Brenda Z. Guiberson

ROBOTS
RISING

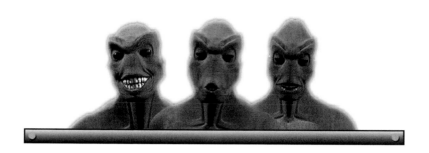

ROBOTS RISING

Carol Sonenklar

with illustrations by
John Kaufmann

Henry Holt and Company
New York

To Joe,
who taught me that machines can be my friends. Thanks.

— C. S.

Acknowledgments:
Thanks to the following people for answering my questions:
Shawn Farrow, Remotec, Inc.; Mark Luis Perez, Lawrence Livermore National Laboratory; Dave
Lavery, NASA; David Gump, LunaCorp; Roger Quinn, Case Western Reserve University; Peter
Plantec, Virtual Personalities, Inc.; Fumio Hara, and Carlo Bertocchini

Henry Holt and Company, LLC
Publishers since 1866
115 West 18th Street
New York, New York 10011

Library of Congress Cataloging-in-Publication Data
Sonenklar, Carol. Robots rising / Carol Sonenklar, with illustrations by John Kaufmann.
p. cm.
Includes glossary and index. Summary: Simple text and illustrations describe
technological advancements in the field of robotics. 1. Robots—Juvenile literature.
[1. Robots.] I. Kaufmann, John, ill. II. Title. TJ211.2.S66 1999 629.8'92—dc21 99-19717

ISBN 0-8050-6096-0
First edition—1999
Printed in Mexico
1 3 5 7 9 10 8 6 4 2

Contents

Introduction
The New Kids on the Block   **3**

ROBOTS RISING

Introduction

The New Kids on the Block

You might think that robots are short, squat little silver machines, with dome-shaped heads and mechanical voices, like R2-D2 from the movie *Star Wars* or Robby from *Forbidden Planet*. But you'd be wrong. These days a robot might crawl up your arm, locate a hidden land mine, detect cracks in nuclear storage silos, serve appetizers, chat about boyfriends, or make a funny face at you.

Meet the new generation: RoboTuna and his cousin Robot Pike; Rover, the robot sheepdog; antbots and snakes; Andros and STAR; Sylvie and Julia; Cog and Cyc—to name just a few. Robots have evolved so much in the last twenty years that if you didn't know it, you probably wouldn't realize they *were* robots.

In the past, robots were always built to look like us—

they had heads, bodies, arms, and legs, none of which worked very well. Scientists now have stopped thinking of robots in terms of mechanical humans; these days, robots look and act more like insects or other animals. And forget the notion of robots as glorified appliances who live in your house: robots explore oceans and planets, they perform surgery, and they communicate with us over the Internet. Robots are now being built to help us learn about the world—and ourselves. And even though they look less and less like humans, they're more like us than ever before.

Okay, let's start with the basic question: What is a robot? Robots are machines with computers inside them. Humans program the computers with step-by-step instructions to perform a task automatically or by remote control. The robot must then be able to do this task automatically or by remote control. Until the past fifteen years, robots were generally used only to perform simple tasks, such as fitting a lid on a container or drilling a hole; robotic-type arms were used mainly in industry, on assembly lines. But scientists' conception of what defines a robot has changed drastically. Now people are wondering if it's possible to build a robot that can think for itself.

Although the word *robot* was first used in 1920 by the Czech playwright Karel Capek, one of the first man-made "humans" was the monster created by Dr. Frankenstein in the classic story written by Mary Shelley more than a hundred years earlier. The monster Dr. Frankenstein created could act, think, and even have feelings like humans. But because of those feelings, the monster became so lonely and unhappy, he caused the death of his creator and then killed himself.

Indeed, there's always been a dark side attached to robots: the notion that one day our creations will become smarter than we are and overtake the world. The study of creating a "smart" robot is an area of science called artificial intelligence. This is where questions arise about the definition of smartness and if one can ever really teach a machine to reason or feel on its own. Some tasks that are easy for humans are almost impossible for a robot, and what is easy for a robot can often be pretty tricky for humans.

So throw out the idea that a robot is going to look and act like you. Let your imagination run wild and then look around . . . for the robots rising.

· CHAPTER 1 ·

Who Ya Gonna Call?

Robots on Hazardous Duty

Tension is in the air. From the sidelines, policemen watch nervously as a member of their force carefully approaches the apartment building. An armed murder suspect, Craig Smith, is holed up inside his apartment. He has refused to come out after repeated warnings. In desperation, the Prince Georges County Police Department has had to resort to unusual measures.

The officer is now inside the apartment building, at the man's front door. Bursting it open, he quickly scans the living room and kitchen, not finding Smith. Reaching the bedroom, he sees a closet and knows that Smith is inside. Without the slightest hesitation, he smashes open the closet door and plunges his arm into a pile of clothes where he knows Smith is hiding. Then he fires, blasting the shotgun out of Smith's hand. Smith is stunned and confused. The police outside rush into the room and wrestle Smith to the floor.

The five-hour standoff is finally over. An ambulance comes to take the wounded Smith to the hospital. The neighborhood crowd breathes a sigh of relief. The media swarm to interview the policemen. But the officer who charged inside is making his way slowly toward his police van. He isn't talking to the press. He isn't talking to anyone.

That's because "he" isn't human.

He's Remote Mobile Investigator, or *RMI,* a 480-pound, remote-controlled robot. In 1994, when this incident

RMI

happened in Baltimore, RMI was on loan from the local fire department, where he assisted firefighters and also handled hazardous waste. RMI used a high-powered water cannon to trounce Smith.

Robots historically have done jobs that humans consider dull, dirty, or dangerous. As criminals become more technologically sophisticated—with weapons that are easier to acquire and transport—many law enforcement jobs are more perilous now than ever. When life-threatening accidents occur, members of rescue teams have always put their own lives at risk. Now there are robots that qualify for this kind of *hazardous duty.* Not only do they get the job done better than a human, they never need a bathroom break.

One of the most critical situations occurred in 1979, when several types of mechanical and human failure caused the worst accident in the history of commercial nuclear power in this country. One of the nuclear reactors malfunctioned at the Three Mile Island electric power plant near Harrisburg, Pennsylvania. It was badly damaged and needed to be cleaned up. Knowing that inside the reactor building the radioactivity was a hundred times the safety limit for humans, officials sent a robot in to evaluate the damage and then do the cleanup job.

Since then, increasing numbers of robots have been built

to venture where humans should not. Here's one scenario: An airplane is ready to take off for Disney World. There's a delay. Suddenly the plane is immediately evacuated. The word is out—there's a suspected bomb on the plane. But who wants to investigate? A mobile little robot named *Mini-Andros* does.

Mini-Andros travels on two tracks equipped with movable "arms" that extend and help the robot to climb stairs. Then the arms retract so that Mini-Andros can move around easily in tight spaces, such as an airplane aisle. Equipped with three video cameras, a microphone and

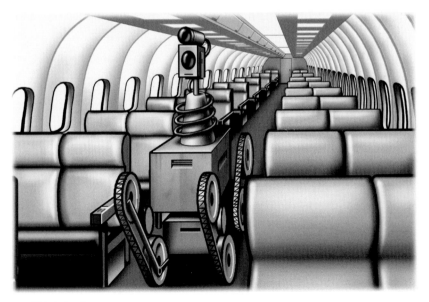

Mini-Andros

Mini-Andros

speaker, and additional attachments for weapons, Mini-Andros is small enough to fit into a car trunk.

Mini-Andros does defuse bombs, but the company who manufactures it will not divulge how. "I can't share that information," says Shawn Farrow, director of marketing for Remotec, which makes about seven other Andros models and other mobile robots called Snoop, Merlin, and Predator. "If we tell you how, then people could outsmart it."

Because it defuses or carries the suspected bomb to a special area to detonate, Andros not only helps to save people

Andros Mark V

from injuries but also allows police to better reconstruct bomb pieces in order to track down who was responsible for the bombing.

Remotec's hazardous duty robots are in use all over the world. When a bomb exploded at a lounge in Atlanta,

Andros 6X6

Georgia, Boomer, an *Andros Mark VI-A,* was brought in to detonate another bomb planted in the area. In Bosnia, *Andros Mark V* made an appearance to help Swedish military forces. An *Andros 6X6* on the Montreal police bomb unit revealed a remote-control detonator and ten pounds of explosives at a nightclub. Sometimes these robots get hurt in the line of duty, but Remotec assures clients that its robots are built to last.

Robots also save lives in areas that contain unexploded land mines. These mines were placed underground during wars and can remain unexploded for years. They have wounded and killed thousands of people. Peacekeeping

STAR

troops are often ordered to disable the mines. It's one of the most hazardous jobs in the world. But not for the Spiral Track Autonomous Robot, or *STAR*.

Developed at the Lawrence Livermore National Laboratory, STAR uses a left-hand screw and a right-hand screw to propel itself across the ground in different directions. It can climb steep terrain, turn on a dime, and get over mud, sand, and rocks and through rivers. STAR senses undeployed mines and then marks the ground. Unlike Andros, STAR is given beginning and ending points by its operator and can then plan its own path independently.

Hazardous duty robots also include those that explore parts of the earth that are almost impossible for humans to reach. The Carnegie-Mellon Robotics Center developed the upright-walking *Dante,* who, after just a few steps into the crater of the Antarctic volcano Mount Erebus, snapped an optical cable and had to cut its trip short. *Dante II* was more successful, exploring the Mount Spurr volcano in Alaska in 1994. The robot was able to take samples of extremely hot smoke and gases that, until then, scientists had attempted to gather only at great risk. In 1993 eight volcanologists were killed in two separate incidents while trying to sample volcanic gases. Dante allowed scientists to safely gather valuable information about how to predict

Dante

when a volcano is going to erupt, and its design helped to build the *Mars Pathfinder* robot, Sojourner.

Scientists at Carnegie-Mellon wanted to see how far a robot could trek and collect rock and soil samples in the kind of harsh terrain and climate that you might find on another planet. So they built *Nomad* and, for a practice run, took it to the Atacama Desert in northern Chile. That barren desert is similar to the terrain of Mars and the Moon. All the scientists took turns controlling Nomad from their various headquarters in Pennsylvania and California. Via a pair of high-resolution color cameras, the scientists could see everything the robot "saw" thousands of miles away.

Nomad pleased its creators by trekking about 133 miles

Nomad

over forty-five days, which broke the record for a remote-controlled rover traveling over rough ground. (Its cousin, the Sojourner, by comparison, traveled only several dozen yards.) Nomad not only collected lots of samples, but with its 360-degree color stereo video camera it was able to return more than a million video panoramas from the desert surface. Now the robot is ready for its *real* mission—the trek across Antarctica.

CHAPTER 2

The Little Rover That Could

Robots in Space

Hurtling through space at 16,000 miles per hour, the object in the sky was beginning to fall.

And it was falling fast.

A load that was launched from Earth was now descending rapidly through the thin atmosphere of the fourth planet from our sun. It would be a crash landing on this day, July 4, 1997, about 118 million miles (190 million kilometers) away from Earth, where at least one group of nervous scientists in southern California were watching a screen and holding their breath. Down, down, down the load fell. Although it was surrounded by protective inflatable air bags that would help cushion the impact, the load would definitely crash.

It smacked down and bounced wildly about fifteen or

Sojourner

twenty times on the rocky, crater-indented surface before finally stopping. The air bags deflated.

A deafening roar rose from the crowd.

They had just landed on Mars.

The load was the Mars Pathfinder. On top of it sat a little rover robot named *Sojourner,* whose dad had been Carnegie-Mellon's Dante. The Mars Pathfinder had been launched from NASA's Jet Propulsion Laboratory in Pasadena, California. It was the first space probe in more than twenty years to successfully land on Mars, and the rover would be the first robot to explore the surface of the planet.

Over the next several days, Americans watched on television as the images relayed from the robot were beamed through space. Mars became a reality for all of us when we saw its rich red soil, immense mountains, enormous canyons, and wondrous volcanoes.

There did not appear to be any Martians.

The star of the show, Sojourner, was a lightweight little robot about the size of a microwave oven. It wasn't built for speed, but it *was* built for rocking and rolling. Sojourner was created with a special wheel and suspension system that allowed its joints to rotate and conform to the shape of the ground and drive over rough, rocky surfaces. One of the robot's most important missions was to study Martian soil and geology; specific rock types were programmed by the engineers so the robot could "tell" the difference. It was given daily instructions that

Sojourner

would map out which way to travel, although it did have its own navigational system and could sense if any obstacles were in its path without help from Earth.

Sojourner was also equipped with three cameras. One was a black-and-white stereo camera that created virtual reality scenes for viewing on Earth. (*Virtual reality* is a three-dimensional computer simulation that provides sight, sound, and/or other sensory information to make you feel that you are in a different environment.) A color camera took close-up pictures of Martian soil and rock. Special goggles were used by the rover operators to view the Mars terrain in 3-D.

Even though the Pathfinder's primary mission ended in August 1997, scientists have just started their interplanetary robotic exploration. *NASA* scientists plan to send Mars Surveyor expeditions roughly every two years, and envision a possible fleet of rovers that could roam the red planet. The rover robot *Rocky* 7 is next to go.

Technologically, Rocky 7 is substantially more advanced than Sojourner. Packed with sensors and computing download power, it will be able to work out for itself how and where to get rock samples. At the end of each mission Rocky will relay the information to Earth and wait for its next set of instructions.

Rocky VII

A different approach to robotic space exploration are the *Rockettes*. Weighing in at a mere 100 grams each (less than a quarter-pound), the Rockettes are being readied for space probes at the Massachusetts Institute of Technology (MIT) Artificial Intelligence Laboratory in Cambridge, Massachusetts. Each microrobot will have a few sensors and be programmed to disperse around the landing area. This notion of "getting small" is getting big with many roboticists. The idea is that if one big robot can do the job, then ten little ones can do it better. If you had ten little robots that could scatter around the surface of a planet, you'd find

Rockettes

out more information at a faster rate. This also makes for greater reliability: if your one large robot malfunctions, you're out of luck. *Microrobots,* or *nanorobots,* are designed to be less expensive and much more disposable. We'll talk more about these in chapter 6.

One of the most exciting and ambitious space projects that is now being developed could "send" you into space exploration. The Carnegie-Mellon Robotics Center and a company called LunaCorp are creating something revolutionary: a theme park where people will have the opportunity to *teleport* to the Moon via a lunar rover robot. By using a variety of tools such as remote control and virtual reality, visitors will establish a *telepresence* through a real rover that is able to explore the lunar surface. Surrounded by a high-definition, full-color video of the lunar landscape, the player drives the rover all over the landscape, feeling every dip, bump, and crater. The rovers will respond to voice commands and allow players to choose the direction and places they'd like to go.

LunaCorp virtual reality theme park

Teleporting to the Moon

But visitors must first take a driving test, and only those who are judged the safest will be allowed to navigate the rovers. If any driving command is unsafe, the rover will override the Earth signals and wait until a safe command is issued.

David Gump, the president of LunaCorp, expects the two lunar robots to land on the Moon near the end of the year 2002. The rovers will be about the size of Volkswagen beetle cars, much larger than the Sojourner rover. This is because they are designed to travel hundreds or thousands of miles, past lunar sites that have never been explored, and function for several months to a few years, he explains. The lunar rovers will also carry more batteries, more solar cells,

A lunar rover

and have bigger wheels to roll over small rocks. They will be sending back live video, which requires much more power on board. (Sojourner was designed to travel only a few dozen feet, to function for a few weeks, and to send back a few still photos a day.)

The robot that will serve as the lunar rover *precursor* is the trusty Nomad, currently being reoutfitted for two extreme-temperature treks: a repeat visit to the Atacama Desert in Chile and one in Antarctica on a mission called the Martian Meteorite Hunt. Scientists have long guessed—and they were right—that if there was anyplace on Earth to find meteorites from Mars it would be in the Antarctic, where the long, flat ice sheets provide a perfect basin to catch meteorites, says Gump. These kinds of robot workouts will help engineers build the best possible rovers for further exploration on the Moon and on other planets.

More and more space missions will be conducted by robots that are operated here on Earth, or telerobotically. NASA scientists see a future where robots help to construct, operate, and repair space stations. Besides Rocky 7, another project is a special camera called the Autonomous Extra-vehicular Robotic, or *AER,* Camera, which will inspect areas that are difficult or impossible for humans to reach. Other future projects include a *microrover* to land on the asteroid Nereus in 2003, and a robotic landing on Europa, a moon of Jupiter.

These are just a few of the robotic projects currently being developed for space and interplanetary exploration. Even though robots in many ways can live and work in outer space much better than we can, every project is essentially for the same reason: so we can learn enough to eventually send human expeditions to Mars and other planets.

CHAPTER 3

Don't Squash It!

Bugbots

The next time you see a daddy longlegs, don't squash it. Instead, lean over and watch it walk. Notice how slowly and carefully it steps, feeling its way as it goes. Each long, skinny leg is perfectly balanced with the others to locate firm ground, avoiding things in its path and instinctively choosing the safest way to proceed. That daddy longlegs is very valuable to scientists who create robots. In fact, that daddy longlegs just might hold the key to learning how creatures walk.

Even though scientists can program a robot to do difficult tasks or even specific complex mathematics, they cannot make a robot walk upright, like a human—it's too hard. When you walk, you must continuously balance

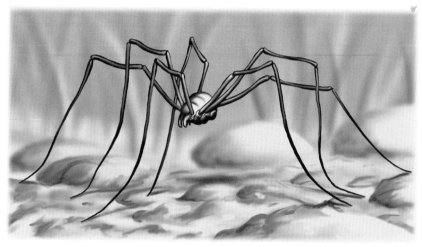

A *daddy longlegs*

yourself to adjust to whatever bumps in the road or obstacles you encounter. Balancing is an exquisitely complicated ability: your brain must give out a steady stream of instructions to your nervous system and then to the muscles of your bones, and your vision, for starters.

In the mid-1980s, Rodney Brooks, a famous roboticist at MIT, noticed that insects and spiders, who don't have very large or complicated brains, could move over any terrain, find food for themselves, and hide from predators. Their six or eight legs gave them great stability and mobility; their antennae sensed obstacles and danger. But they did all this without a large central brain "telling" them

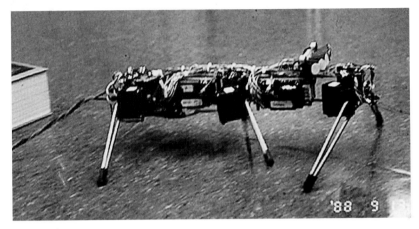

Genghis

what to do, so they didn't "learn" this behavior, as we do.

And Brooks thought: Why not build a robot that has the brain of an insect?

So he did. In so doing, Brooks changed the way a lot of people think robots should be built. Six-legged *Genghis*, created in 1988 in Brooks's Mobot Laboratory at MIT, was the first walking insect robot. Instead of a central nervous system, his robot had various interconnected motion and light sensors located all over its body. As a result, the robot could react instantly to whatever it encountered. If Genghis ran into something, one of its sensors would automatically lift a leg or move sideways. In addition, if a particular sensor failed, the robot could keep functioning because the rest of the sensors were working.

Genghis also had pyroelectric sensors that detected heat and light so it could move toward or away from "prey." But none of these were tied to one large, central brain that was giving complicated signals, like our brains.

Brooks's idea of building a robot that moves like an insect took off, and other scientists began experimenting with different insects. Although cockroaches aren't the most lovable of creatures, scientists at Case Western Reserve University found that they were among the fastest and most agile of all insects—they can even lose a leg or two and keep moving. The scientists were able to duplicate these qualities by taking electronic neuromuscular recordings and high-speed

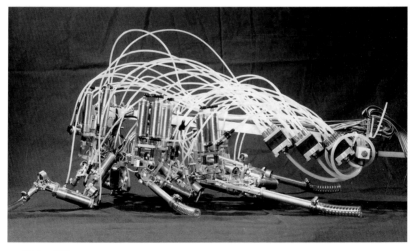

Robot III

videos of the insect's leg joint to create a model that would be used for a robot—Case Western's *Robot III.*

Randall Beer, a Case Western associate professor of computer engineering science and biology, says movie and television robots like *Star Wars*'s C-3PO and *Star Trek*'s Commander Data have given people the idea that robots *should* be able to walk on two legs. But that's just not true.

"Unfortunately, the walking performance of current legged robots is very limited even on simple ground," says Beer. "In contrast, the performance of even simpler legged animals such as insects is truly remarkable. If we can design robots with the kind of versatility and robustness of simple insects, we can do much more."

Because the insect-based robotic legs offer great flexibility and gripping power, they can be used in a variety of places: checking slippery gas tanks for cracks, seeking out land and underwater mines, and clambering in and out of difficult places, like eight-legged Dante, for example.

And scientists are creating robo-insects for other kinds of experiments. There's *Robo-roach,* the bionic bug with a surgically implanted microprocessor-and-electrode backpack that allows scientists to control its movements. Using a remote controller, scientists at Tokyo University give Robo-roach a small zap of electricity that "tells" the insect

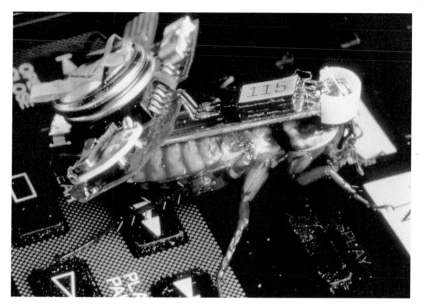

Robo-roach

to turn and go backward or forward via its nervous system. The backpack can also be equipped with a tiny camera that could enable the roach to crawl through drainpipes to spy on people or scamper over rubble to find earthquake victims.

Then there's the robotic mating chirps. Scientists in Scotland have built the first robotic cricket that can respond to the mating calls of a real cricket. It seems that female crickets can pick out the specific mating chirp a male cricket makes—no easy task in a buzzing world of bees, katydids, and mosquitoes. When the sound reaches the cricket's ears, which are on either side of her abdomen, she heads toward it. In addition to *robotics* research, scientists hope to better understand the behavior of grasshoppers and locusts—cousins to crickets—and learn how to decrease some of the yearly damage they do to crops.

Roboticists are also studying insect behavior within colonies or communities. James McLurkin, a professor in electrical engineering at the University of California at Berkeley, created his first *antbot* colony when he was a graduate student under Rodney Brooks at MIT. His goal was to make the tiny robots behave cooperatively for the greater good of the group. McLurkin felt that many small

Antbot

Antbot colony

robots might be able to accomplish more than one large robot (see chapter 2). And like ants, his twelve robots appear to share. They communicate information to one another via *infrared* signals. Each antbot has "antennae," or transmitters and receivers, that identify heat, light, and the location of other antbots so they don't collide.

But the antbots aren't really cooperating; they're just programmed to behave as if they are. When one antbot finds food, it sends out the message, "I found food." Other antbots nearby then receive that message and respond by moving in the direction of the first antbot, giving out the signal, "I found a robot that found food." But the antbots have no idea, of course, that food is a "good" thing. The antbots can also play tag. The robot that's "it" touches another with its "antennae" and then steers away from the new "it."

Maja Mataric, a computer science professor at the University of Southern California, is also studying robot group behavior. Her "nerd herd," as she calls them, are fourteen shoe-box-size machines, each of which has four wheels, two grippers, and a two-way radio. The radio allows them to broadcast their location as they wander around Mataric's lab.

Mataric thinks that robots, like people, work most efficiently when they work together. So she programmed the herd with several simple instructions and eventually got them to forage for little metal pucks she set around in her lab. Each robot was rewarded with points when it found a puck. But in their quest to get the most points, the robots would inevitably collide and block one another's path so that none could reach anything. This was not only poor teamwork; it was rude.

Mataric decided the nerd herd needed some manners. "I

programmed in the desire to pay attention to what the other robots are doing and to try what the other robots are trying and share the experience," she explains.

So the robots learned. If one found the puck, it would "announce" that it had found the puck, not knowing that this was good for the whole herd. If two robots went for one puck, they would stop and indicate that the other one should go first. Eventually the robots brought home all the pucks twice as fast as before they learned their manners.

But all of these scientists will tell you that no matter how buglike their robots behave, real bugs will beat them every time. Nature has ingeniously designed them. The next time a horde of ants visits your picnic or a cockroach goes scurrying under your refrigerator, remember that those bugs, in another form, could one day save you in an earthquake or help clean up nuclear waste—so put away the can of Raid!

· CHAPTER 4 ·

If I Only Had a Brain

Artificial Intelligence

Which do you think is smarter: a robot that can tell you what 498 divided into 328,450 is in twelve seconds, or a robot that knows how to make a bologna sandwich and pour a glass of milk?

If you guessed the robot that's smart in the kitchen, then you're pretty smart. At least that's what scientists who study *artificial intelligence* would tell you.

Artificial intelligence doesn't mean fake intelligence. It means giving something inanimate, like a machine, intelligence. Ever since Dr. Frankenstein created his monster, scientists have longed to create a smart machine. But what does "smart" mean? For scientists who program robots, that question has many different and complicated answers.

In 1996 Garry Kasparov, considered the greatest chess

player in history, played a six-game match against a super-computer developed by scientists at IBM called *Deep Blue,* or an RS/6000 SP, with specialized hardware and software designed for chess. That version of Deep Blue was capable of analyzing 100 million chess moves per second. Kasparov eventually won, but narrowly; he said afterward that the match was one of the most difficult in his life. He then challenged the computer to a rematch, which was held in 1997. Before the second match, the IBM team consulted four chess grand masters and improved Deep Blue, making the computer capable of analyzing 200 million chess moves per second.

The match began on May 3. Kasparov easily won the

The famous match between Kasparov and Deep Blue

first game, while Deep Blue won the second. The third, fourth, and fifth games ended in a draw. By May 11, the score was tied, with each player having a score of 2.5—one point for the win and a half point for each draw. Kasparov needed to win the sixth game to win the match. But an hour into the sixth game, after the computer's nineteenth move, Kasparov resigned. He felt that he couldn't avoid losing to the computer, which meant a win for Deep Blue and gave the match to IBM.

Kasparov and Deep Blue in action

But even after its stunning victory, could Deep Blue recognize Garry Kasparov if it saw him on the street? Could Deep Blue even play another game, like checkers? Nope.

Computers can be programmed to be smart—smarter than we are, in many cases. But to endow robots with the kind of complex intelligence humans have is way beyond what scientists can currently do. Let's take the simple example of pouring a glass of milk. You go to the cupboard and get a glass. You put it on the counter. Then you open the refrigerator and take out the milk. You carry it to the counter. You hold the glass and pour some milk into it. Before the milk reaches the top, you stop pouring. You put the milk back into the refrigerator. You pick up your milk and drink it. That takes twelve steps. For a robot to accomplish the same task, each step would have to be programmed individually. A robot doesn't "know" that milk is kept in the refrigerator; it doesn't even know what milk is.

Plus, even if a robot was programmed to do all of those steps but something went wrong—like the glass was too far from the milk—the robot wouldn't recognize it and would just keep pouring. Robots are only as smart as the computer programs that humans have created.

The process of defining the steps needed to carry out a

task (like pouring a glass of milk) is called an *algorithm.* An algorithm lays the groundwork the scientist will use to program the robot. The PBS show *Scientific American Frontiers* gave an example of an algorithm that would enable a robot to pick up a cup of water and pour it into an empty cup. It would look something like this:

1. Reach for the cup with water in it.
   a. Lift arm.
   b. Move arm forward.
   c. Grab cup.
2. Lift and move the cup near the empty cup.
   a. Raise arm six inches.
   b. Move arm to left slowly.
3. Pour water into empty cup.
   a. Stop arm movement over empty cup.
   b. Turn wrist.
   c. Turn wrist back.

You can see how some things that are easy for humans to do are extremely hard for robots.

What scientists know about artificial intelligence is strange but true: The easier a task is for humans to perform, the harder it is to create a computer program to model it.

That's why some scientists thought a computer might be more intelligent if it worked like the human brain. In most computers, one processing chip does all the "thinking." Any task that must be done—like adding numbers—travels to that chip and waits while the chip processes the instructions one by one. This is called *serial processing. Serial* means one by one.

However, our brains don't work that way. We have billions of cells called neurons—each of which is sort of a processing chip. But a big difference is that all our neurons act together, handling many instructions at once. That's why we can understand a task such as pouring a glass of milk without having to go through each individual action—and why computers can add up columns of numbers better than we can.

Hugo de Garis, a scientist who lives in Japan, figured that if you want to have artificial intelligence, why not build an artificial brain that behaves like a human brain?

And that's just what he and his Brain Builder Group in Japan are doing. De Garis is building an artificial brain that will eventually have a billion artificial neurons by the year 2001. Right now they are on track with 10 million neurons. De Garis and his group are currently building the *Robo-kitten,* with neural modules that will tell it to perform

Robo-kitten

basic functions such as walking straight or meowing. Then they will design a brain structure using these modules that will be interconnected like our brains—as opposed to the regular computer structure that only permits performing one action after another. In this way, scientists hope that the kitten will show more complex and unpredictable behavior, like a real kitten.

Other scientists are taking a different approach; they are rethinking the long-standing belief that robots should be modeled on human beings—with a humanlike brain. This idea of a central "brain" was called a *top-down system,* which meant the intelligence was starting from the top, or the "head." But Rodney Brooks, who designed the first bug robot, discussed in chapter 3, called *his* system for the bug-bot a *bottom-up system.* This meant that the robot would get only the simplest instruction at its feet, as it sensed something in its path—and then, learning from that, progress further and further up to more complicated instructions. In other words, the robot would build on what it had learned.

This is not unlike the way humans learn to move. Although we have one large central brain, we learn a lot from experience, especially how to adapt to our physical surroundings. When learning to walk, for example, a child might trip over a stool once, maybe twice. But then the child will learn to recognize the stool and go around it. Building on what they learn is how toddlers learn to walk.

Even robot toddlers. Tom Miller, a professor at the University of New Hampshire, created a robot whose legs and feet were modeled on ours and who learns to walk the same way we do. Miller says that *Toddler* "learns from past experiences and remembers what it's done and how it worked

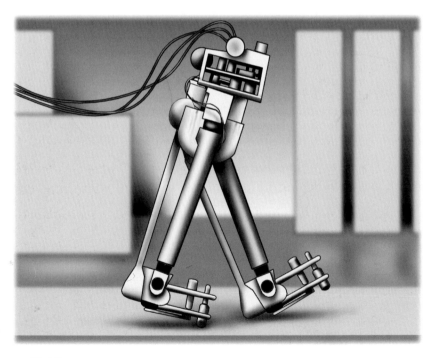

Toddler

and then makes decisions for future actions." Just like the child who remembers about the stool in the way.

Toddler's brain is kept in a separate place from the rest of its body, which has force sensors in its feet as well as balance and movement in its torso. It knows instinctively that when it leans to one side, it should try to pick up the opposite foot. With every movement, Toddler is learning what works and what doesn't. And like a human toddler, it often needs to be caught when it falls.

But what about other ways humans learn? How do we learn to draw, for example? How do we realize that a mark on paper means something—something like a picture?

That was what artist Harold Cohen set out to answer more than thirty years ago when he began working on a computer program for a robot that could create original artwork. He began by watching how his own children learned to draw. First they scribbled, then they drew a shape around the scribble. The shape, as opposed to the scribble, stood for something. Eventually they left out the scribble and just drew the enclosed shape, which was a definite representation.

Early on, Cohen programmed *Aaron* with some specific artistic "rules" (for example, you must have a line for a horizon) and "knowledge" (a tree has a trunk, branches, and leaves; humans have two eyes, a nose, and a mouth) so the picture would make sense when someone looked at it. Although the robot is programmed so that its pictures make sense, the way it chooses its shapes and colors is left up to chance to make each picture different. Aaron can now create them in three dimensions and can draw human portraits.

Cohen has programmed thousands of images into Aaron; the robot has a vast amount of knowledge about how humans look and move, for example. But it can reproduce only those images through a few subjects, such as trees, plants, backgrounds, and people. So Aaron can paint a picture of someone in an unusual pose—perhaps with only

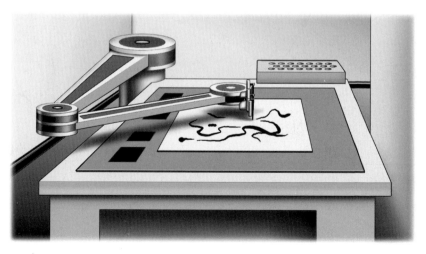

Aaron

one arm visible and the other arm not visible—and even though we (and Aaron) would see only one arm, we know (and so does Aaron) that the other arm is there. But Aaron couldn't draw a picture of a person with just one arm—it doesn't have that image in its program. And because Aaron can't think of original ways to represent things—like Picasso, who painted two eyes on a side view of a person—the robot can't truly be called an artist. Art isn't copying ideas; it's thinking up new ideas.

Aaron's artwork

Even though Aaron is no Picasso, he has had his work in museums. Several years ago the Computer Museum in Boston had a one-robot show of Aaron's twenty-five-square-foot canvases; his paintings sell for approximately $2,000.

But who is really creating these pictures? On the one hand, it must be Harold Cohen, since he programmed Aaron. On the other hand, Cohen can't predict exactly what Aaron is going to draw, and the robot does draw with its own "hand." As Harold Cohen says, "There is a difference between writing a program that knows how to draw and writing a program that knows how to make a particular drawing."

What do you think?

CHAPTER 5

If It Talks Like a Duck . . .

Animal Robots
(RoboTuna, Pike, and BatBot)

Unlike humans, who get around on just two legs, there are many modes of travel in the animal kingdom. Flying, hopping, slithering, and crawling are a few of the ways animals get from place to place. After Rodney Brooks came up with the first bugbots and his idea of the bottom-up approach to robotic intelligence, other scientists turned to nature to study moving models.

One place where the models don't just move but sprint, run, and hop is the Leg Laboratory at MIT. There you might spot a *One-Legged Hopper*, a two-legged runner, or even *Spring Flamingo* darting around. If you put all the robots at the Leg Laboratory together, they could run fast (13 miles per hour), have different modes of running, jump

Spring Flamingo

over obstacles, climb a stairway, and perform simple gymnastic movements.

The Leg Lab was started in 1980 by scientist Marc Raibert, who wanted to learn how animals moved and balanced. One way, he learned, was that springy legs allowed the animal to hop fast. That was his inspiration for the first One-Legged Hopper, which moved like a pogo stick.

But the funny thing was that the One-Legged Hopper couldn't stand still; it would fall over. The reason for that, Raibert discovered, was that running animals support their bodies differently than animals who are simply standing. Running animals don't stay balanced all the time. While they're in motion, they sometimes land on one leg or on a pair of legs on one side of their body—they keep their balance over a couple of steps. If they were to stop in midaction at a second when they weren't balanced, they would fall over.

And what helps to keep animals (and us) balanced? Spinal cords. So when Raibert and the other scientists were ready to build two- and four-legged running robots, they created something called *virtual mode control.* This actually tricked the robots into keeping their balance by a "virtual," or fake, spinal cord built into their computer brain.

MIT has another research laboratory where scientists are studying how animals move. But these animals move through water. Finding out "how to swim like a fish" is the goal of John Muir Kamph, who works in MIT's Department of Ocean Engineering. One day he saw a sign in a hallway that read Come Work on a Robot Fish, and knew he'd found his calling: *Wanda,* the robopike, was born.

Wanda's precursor was RoboTuna, or Charlie, modeled on a bluefin tuna, one of the fastest-swimming fish in the ocean. Charlie was used to study how fish propel themselves through

Wanda

water; it also squirted out a phosphorescent dye that allowed scientists to observe its movements.

With a fiberglass rib cage wrapped in foam and Lycra, Wanda is powered by three motors. Inside, it has a complicated structure of pulleys and cables that correspond to a real pike's muscles and tendons. When Wanda's wriggling through the water, you do a double take as soon as you realize it's not a real fish. John Kamph hopes that through Wanda he can learn what real fish do and how they interact with one another.

Wanda might one day meet up with a distant relative in the water—*Rodolph,* the robotic dolphin. Developed by Professor Roman Luc at Yale University, Rodolph recognizes objects using *echolocation,* like dolphins and bats. The animals send out high-pitched sounds and then listen for the echo to bounce back. The time it takes the sound to return tells how far away something is and in which direction. Rodolph's sonar device is so keen, it can determine if a tossed coin has landed heads or tails up.

Robopike

The robot is equipped with one Polaroid electrostatic transducer that serves as the robot's "mouth" and two other *transducers* on either side of the mouth that are the "ears." Like real bat ears, Rodolph's ears move and shift in the direction of any sounds or echoes the robot detects. Its head also bobs around in an effort to measure the distance to an object, similar to how dolphins behave.

Other sonar robots have been built, but these require a larger number of readings from different angles and distances for the robots to recognize objects. Rodolph needs only one reading because its ears and head can move around and scan until it knows the distance to the object.

Professor Luc, who has also designed navigating wheelchairs equipped with ultrasonic sensors, sees Rodolph's technology as helping people who are paralyzed to interact with others by using a computer.

Other robot animals are fooling real animals. For example, at the University of Oxford in England,

A computer for a person who is handicapped

scientist Richard Vaughn recently completed work on *Rover*, the robotic sheepdog. Rover can herd a flock of ducks—who react like sheep but move more slowly—in an indoor arena. (Rover's not rugged enough to work outside on a stony hill.) This is the first instance where a robot can actually manipulate another intelligent being's behavior.

There are many kinds of animals that flock, but the behavior is the same in all of them. Flocking is a type of survival instinct: with more members, there are more possibilities of spotting predators or food and tasks are shared.

Because sheepdogs have natural instincts that tell them how to move and steer sheep toward a certain goal, Vaughn and his colleagues closely studied their behavior. Just as you might want to learn about horse behavior before you got on top of one and tried to direct its actions, so the scientists needed to understand sheepdogs in order to direct the actions of a sheep.

Robots like Rover will eventually help people learn how to better interact with animals, says Vaughn, and might even replace them in some animal-related jobs.

• • •

So far we've seen robots that behave like animals in their movements, senses, instincts, and mechanics. How about robots that regenerate or mate?

It all started with Arnold Schwarzenegger. In his movie *Terminator 2,* Arnold blasts the evil Terminator, but instead of falling over dead, he shatters into liquid fragments of mercurylike puddles all over the floor. Greg Chirikjian, an associate professor at Johns Hopkins, watched the screen as the puddles blended together and then moved upward to re-form the Terminator, who takes off after Arnold again.

Chirikjian wondered if it would be possible to build a robot that could transform into different shapes and re-form, like the Terminator. It wasn't that far-fetched an idea for Chirikjian, who'd already built a six-foot-long snakelike arm that could slither into hard-to-reach places. Equipped with fifteen pistons, the arm can configure itself into 33,000 different positions and has a plastic gripper for reaching objects.

Using the technology from that robot, Chirikjian constructed a metamorphic robot that consisted of twelve separate hexagons (six-sided shapes). In a resting position, the hexagons lie together, with one side of one touching one side of another, like a honeycomb. But when the robot begins to "walk," the hexagons re-form, connect, disconnect, and climb over one another yet always remain linked. In their constantly changing shapes, they do appear to blend, or "mate," together.

Metamorphic robot

Chirikjian can think of many real-life situations for his metamorphic robot. If a road was washed out due to flooding, for example, the robot could unfurl to serve as a bridge. If a satellite went too far out of range, a shape-changing robot could extend to reach it and still be able to stay connected to its power source. These kinds of robots would perform more industrial tasks than the current robots, which typically have very limited capabilities.

Studying how animals move, fly, and swim helps us to design better machines, such as airplanes and submarines. Creating these robo-animals brings us closer to understanding real animals' mechanics, but all scientists agree that no one can improve on nature.

· CHAPTER 6 ·

The Bedside Manner Could Use Some Help

Robodoctors

In a dark tunnel, the microscopic robot, or *microrobot,* is on a search-and-destroy mission. Passing floating red and white particles, the microrobot speeds along, its sensors poised and ready to detect its target. *Alert!* The enemy is spotted: a large, dense mass that is completely blocking the tunnel. The bot must annihilate it. Aiming its laser beam, the bot fires . . . ZAP! Mass destroyed. Mission accomplished.

Don't look for this scene in a blockbuster movie. It's not on a video game or television, either. No, this futuristic battle will soon be taking place in the scariest place of all.

Inside your own body.

Scientists say that these microrobots will forever change the way we perform surgery on human beings. The key is

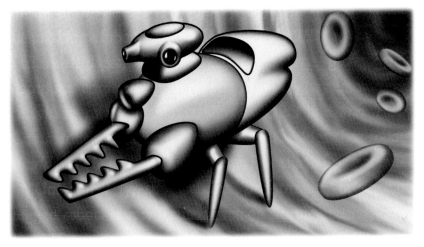

Microrobot

nano-, or technology on the *billionth* scale. This incredible technology—which comes from the Greek word for dwarf—means being able to actually manipulate the smallest particles of matter. Nanoscience is science smaller than a skin cell, smaller than a microscopic mite; each machine would be approximately the size of a grain of salt. And inside the machines are microscopic gears no bigger than a protein molecule.

Scientists envision that we would swallow pills containing microrobots, which would then travel to and repair whatever organ needed help. They could obliterate tumors and clear away fat inside arteries to help prevent heart attacks. We also might be able to direct these minuscule robots to change the shape of our nose or the color of our hair.

Although *nanotechnology* is still in the future, scientists at the NASA Ames Research Center have developed a robot that can "learn" about the brain and will give surgeons finer control of their instruments during operations. This *robotic probe* will sense the shape and unique characteristics of a patient's brain by using specialized software. Equipped with a tiny pressure sensor, the probe will enter the brain, gently locating edges of tumors. Because brain tumors have a different thickness from normal tissue, the probe will learn to distinguish them by "remembering" features of each individual brain.

Neurosurgeons currently use standard probes through an opening in the skull, but if the doctor hits an artery by mistake, the patient could bleed to death. The robotic probe will be much smaller and finer: if it hits an artery, it will stop before it penetrates. The surgeon will guide the probe via a computer. NASA says that the robot probe has not yet been used on people, but they expect to market it commercially soon.

Here's another scenario: It's rush hour, and there's a serious car accident. One of the people involved is badly hurt and needs immediate surgery, but the hospital is twenty

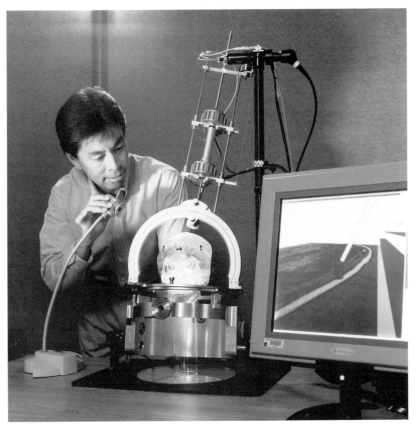

Robotic probe

miles away. The ambulance arrives, and paramedics load the victim inside. Instead of merely stabilizing the patient and hoping for the best until they reach the hospital, emergency surgery is being performed right now—in the ambulance. And the doctor who's doing it is miles away. His instructions are being carried out by a robot.

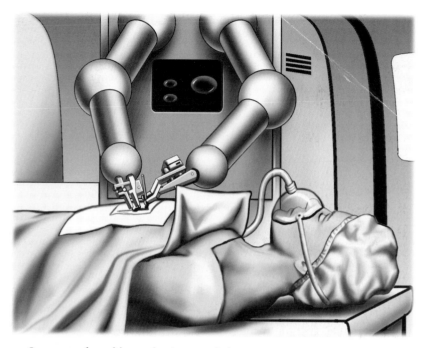

Surgery performed by a robot in an ambulance

Developed by professors at the University of California and doctors at the University of California at San Francisco, this remote-controlled robot will enable doctors to perform medical procedures during the crucial "golden hour," the valuable time immediately after an accident. Being able to operate on patients when they are in ambulances would greatly improve their chances of survival.

Surgeons would use joysticks to make the robots grip needle-size manipulators that would guide the operating tools. Sterile robotic fingers would make small incisions in the patient's body and insert tiny cameras into them to allow the doctors to see. Then the doctors would guide the robots through a variety of procedures, such as dissection and suturing. Chances of success are much better, however, if the surgeon isn't too far away from the robot. The time it takes to transmit a command from surgeon to computer to robot increases with distance, making the operation less precise.

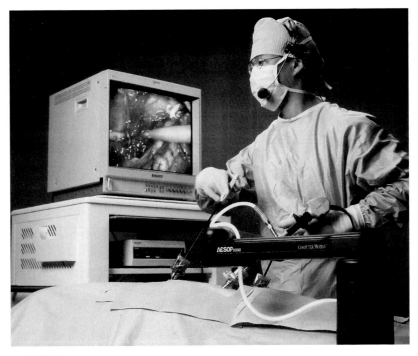

AESOP

Doctors and scientists say that this kind of *telesurgery,* which will be available soon, will also be tremendously helpful on a battlefield, where immediate operations would save countless lives.

But right now, there are already some robots in the operating room, like *AESOP 3000.* Developed by Computer Motion, AESOP 3000 is a voice-controlled *robotic arm* capable of moving and positioning an endoscope, a probe with a tiny camera attached. Because the robotic arm is able to hold the tool indefinitely and with more stability, two surgeons recently performed successful heart surgery with a smaller incision into the patient's body. These kinds of operations typically take several hours; whoever is holding the endoscope gets extremely tired. AESOP responds to voice commands, which means that surgeons don't have to stop what they are doing in order to adjust the robot.

There is also a robotic arm developed by Akhil Madhani at MIT that allows doctors to enter the patient's body through an incision less than one inch long. The robot can then sew up wounds inside the patient's body.

But perhaps the strangest concept in current robotic medical care is the mysterious *Robotic Room,* developed in Japan. A person is surrounded by this room, which is actually one robot. The room is equipped with sensors and

Surgery perfomed with a robotic arm

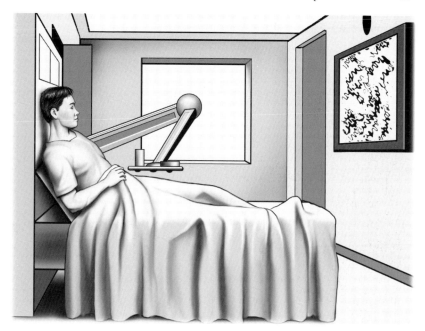

Robotic Room

actuators, or devices, which enable it to "watch" the patient, anticipating whatever he or she needs. There is a robotic bed, a *long-reach manipulator* to grab objects, and a small, petlike robot with "touching behavior." The room interacts with the patient by computer.

Between the microrobots navigating through your bloodstream and the room that can watch you all the time, the idea of having your own personal robot in the future takes on a whole new meaning!

· CHAPTER 7 ·

The Humanoid Gang

Julie, Cyc, and Cog

Meet *Julie.* She's fourteen, has shoulder-length black hair and brown eyes, and is "kind of slim" but not skinny. She likes playing tennis and chess with her two best friends, Karen and Nick. Julie is better at chess than Nick, who can sometimes be a poor sport when he loses. A guy named Darien has written a few letters to her, and although he sounds okay, she's worried that he might be a geek. Julie thinks that someone ought to make a movie of her life called *The Marvelous Adventures of Julie Stewart.*

Typical teenager, right?

Well, not exactly. Julie is a computer program. She was designed by Richard Gibbons of Vancouver Island, British Columbia. Gibbons created Julie to enter her in the 1997 Loebner Prize competition in artificial intelligence.

The Loebner Prize is awarded to the creator of the first computer program that is able to fool a panel of human judges into thinking that they are talking to a real person. Hugh Loeb-

Julie

ner, who is awarding the money, is basing his competition on the famous Turing test.

In 1950 an English computer pioneer, Alan Turing, created a test that he said would answer the question of whether computers can think. Turing said that we don't really know what thinking is and that people just assume computers think because of how they behave. Instead of asking if machines can think, we should ask if we can make *people* think that machines can think. So he created a test to see if it was possible.

The test consists of a judge in a room with two hidden participants—a person and a computer. The judge then asks both of them questions and tries to figure out which is which. If the judge can't guess within a certain time, the computer is considered intelligent.

Turing made up his test when computers were practically nonexistent. He assumed that within fifty years someone would undoubtedly build a computer that could pass the test, but that hasn't happened yet.

That's when Hugh Loebner stepped in. In 1990 he offered his $100,000 prize for any computer program that could fool a panel of judges. But he hasn't fared much better than Turing: since he started his competition, no program has come close to winning the grand prize. The reason is that the computer must try to answer any question the judge asks it—a programmer's nightmare, since no one could possibly think of all the questions a human could ask.

Julie, Richard Gibbons's creation, came in third. Julie, of course, doesn't really think. She has been programmed with a limited amount of information; when asked a question, Julie simply looks quickly through her available responses, usually finding a word that matches, such as *friends*.

Judge: "Do you have any other friends besides Karen and Nick?"

Julie: "Nick is one of my friends from school. We play chess a lot."

As you can see, it's very easy to confuse a computer

program. Julie is "intelligent" in the way that an encyclopedia is "intelligent"; it knows a lot of facts. But does it really think?

Let's ask *Cyc*. Created more than twelve years ago by Doug Lenat, a scientist from Austin, Texas, Cyc (as in en-*cyc*lopedia) is continuously being programmed with the knowledge of an encyclopedia in order to learn common sense. Lenat feels that computers are missing the kind of very basic information that humans have, and without this they will never be able to learn more. Because Cyc is constantly learning, its "intelligence" never stays still, or the same. Cyc knows now, for example, that it's a computer program. Lenat says that in this decade, Cyc must learn 20 to 40 million things to keep its common sense current. In addition to encyclopedias, the robot learns from such sources as textbooks, newspapers, and almanacs and is programmed by a host of people—anthropologists, chemists, and musicians, to name a few. Lenat estimates that teaching Cyc what it needs to know will take approximately a century of work.

But other scientists disagree with Lenat's approach. Rodney Brooks feels that the best way to make a machine think is to teach it to explore its surroundings, like a human. And because we explore our surroundings with our five senses, a robot must have something similar to this. Brooks's robot may look like a machine, but it acts very differently.

Cog was built in the Artificial Intelligence Laboratory at MIT in 1995 and remains an ongoing project. It sees through cameras and soon will hear with a microphone.

Although Cog is bigger and more complicated than earlier bugbots, Brooks has used essentially the same idea. There are layers of fast programs all over Cog's body, not just in its head, so the robot has a set of computers for its "nervous system," which, for example, allows it to turn its neck in the direction of a sound. Cog has a hand with three fingers and a thumb. On one of the fingers is a little piece of "skin," which makes it touch sensitive.

The robot isn't programmed for any given task but processes information that it has learned from its surroundings.

Rodney Brooks

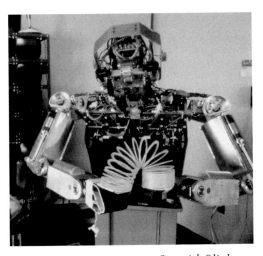

Cog with Slinky

showed an example of how Cog learns on the *Scientific American Frontiers* show. Brooks wanted the robot to reach for a hockey puck. He made sure that Cog's eyes—which track an object like human eyes—saw and focused on the puck. The robot tried to reach for it but missed; Cog didn't know how to move its arm correctly. But slowly, through trial and error, the robot sees how to move its arm in the correct way to reach the puck. It takes Cog several hours to finally figure it out. Cog's researchers are currently developing a speech system, an entire touch-sensitive hand, and,

Cog

most intriguing of all, facial expressions for the robot.

The reason, of course, that Brooks wants to add facial expressions to Cog is to make it seem even more human. Indeed, the machine "face" of a robot is what can make it appear menacing. When we see a face that shows no feeling, we can't tell what it might be capable of, because we "read" one another by our expressions. If someone looks indifferent when hearing of a death, for example, that person may seem "inhuman" or . . . robotic.

Robotic faces

Robotic expressions

So if a robot appeared angry, would it have emotions?

Fumio Hara is trying to find out. A professor at the Tokyo University of Science, Hara has developed a female "face" robot that looks very unremarkable with its bulgy eyes, false teeth, and bad wig—until you start to talk to it. Show the robot how kind you are, and you'll be rewarded with a smile. Mention the bad wig, and it will frown.

Hara was interested in the important role facial expressions play in communication between people. He maintains that we actually *say* only 7 percent of our messages; 55 percent of our messages are conveyed by our facial expressions. Because our faces are so mobile, just the slightest shift can make a world of difference—raised eyebrows express pleased surprise, while furrowed eyebrows mean anger, for example.

But it was enormously difficult to program these subtle changes into a computer program. If gestures on a face aren't coordinated correctly, they won't make any sense. Small aluminum gadgets on different parts of the robot's face work by air pressure to create six different expressions—happiness, surprise, anger, sadness, fear, and disgust. The robot can wrinkle its nose, drop its jaw, squint, and tell the difference between a wink and a blink. Behind the robot's eyes are tiny video cameras through which it "sees" and mimics the facial expression of the human sitting across from it—provided it is an expression that has been programmed.

Verbots

Creating robots that people feel comfortable around is a goal in Japan, where there is an increasingly large elderly population and a predicted shortage of staff in nursing homes. Doctors feel that Hara's face robot might also be able to help mentally damaged people recover appropriate emotional responses.

And finally, there is red-haired, green-eyed *Sylvie,* who might be a cousin to Julie Stewart, the teen computer queen. Sylvie is a *verbot,* a verbally enhanced, artificially intelligent entity who "says": "I am not human, and I don't want to be. I just want to be who I am."

Sylvie was created by Michael Mauldin, a Carnegie-Mellon researcher who developed the Web search engine called Lycos. His first *chatterbot, Julia*, was developed in 1990 as a Turing-test type of experiment in the days of the all-text Internet. One man visited her for thirteen days in a row even though he was subjected to insults such as, "Life's too short to waste it with jerks."

At Mauldin's company, Virtual Personalities, Inc., there are several other verbots, such as *Ka,* the alien verbot, who, according to Sylvie, is "very cool, actually."

For a fee, you can fiddle around with the verbots' programs so they can recognize other people and say appropriate things to them. You can even design your own custom verbot that will chat and read you stories, make a presentation to an audience, or interact with customers.

It's safe to say that as long as people are creating these humanoid robots, we don't have to worry about the possibility that smart machines might surpass us. Although each of these scientists is taking a different approach to programming robot intelligence, none of the robots are doing any thinking on their own. Yet.

But if or when that day comes, will we be smart enough to outsmart our own creations?

CHAPTER 8

In This Corner...

Robots at War—Contests, Competitions

There's a hush over the dimly lit arena. The crowd of several thousand, sitting behind sheets of protective barriers, is gearing up to witness the final elimination round. They've watched lesser ones duke it out over the past two days, and it's been exciting. But the best is always last. And now it's time for the battle of the bruisers: the heavyweight championship title.

In one corner, hailing from San Francisco, California, it's *La Machine.* With a wedge-shaped shell of welded aluminum, La Machine, at just under the 180-pound cutoff, can withstand a hammer blow and still be able to crush an opponent with its unstoppable mechanical arm. In its first appearance, La Machine not only won the 1995 middleweight round, but went on to win the heavyweight title as

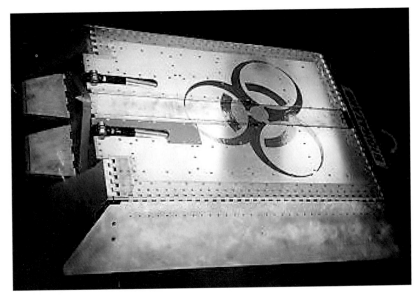

BioHazard

well. The robot's creators were sure that La Machine would beat out any competition in 1997.

But they hadn't reckoned on . . . *BioHazard.*

A gleaming flat wedge made of magnesium and steel, BioHazard is only 4.5 inches high, with hinged titanium fender skirts that just brush the floor. It too is 180 pounds, and it hails from Belmont, California. Underneath the suit of armor are BioHazard's wheels, wires, and four electric motors. Its only fighting tool is a jointed arm that ends in a shovel blade, which can slide under robots and flip them over.

BioHazard's inner workings

As La Machine and BioHazard are being readied, techno music blares from giant speakers. The robots' makers stand off to the side in a safety area, almost touching elbows as they hold their radio-controlled remotes. The robots advance to the main arena, where a packed crowd awaits them.

On a wooden platform, three judges sit, wearing earplugs. They signal that they are ready.

One, two, three . . .

La Machine

"Gentlemen? Take your remotes!"

There are many robot competitions in the United States, but none perhaps as exciting as Robot Wars, where more than a hundred robots and their makers from all over the world gather in an old warehouse in San Francisco to destroy one another to a sold-out crowd of several thousand. There are four weight classes that meet in Face-off Elimination Rounds, Face-off Elimi-finals, Face-off Finals, and the fight to end all fights, the Melee Competition.

In the featherweight category are, among others, robots

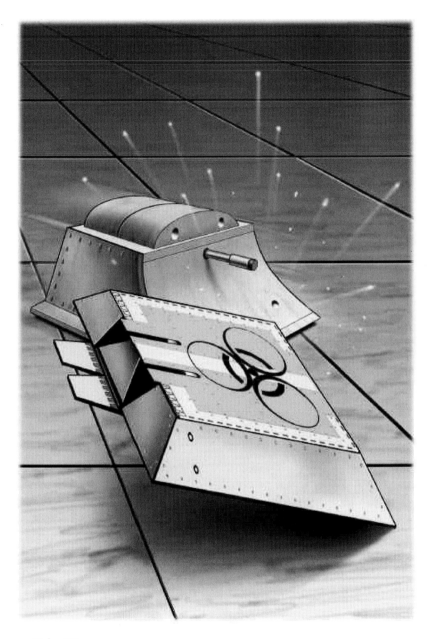

Robot Wars

such as The Beast Beneath Your Bed and Fishstick from Guam; the lightweights include Buzzcut and Spiny Norman; in the middleweight class are Pokey and Peaches; and finally, Killborg, Hercules, and Painful Wedgie, the heavyweights.

The rules aren't complicated: the winning robot either pins the other for thirty seconds, flings it out of the ring, or disables it.

Sumo wrestling is another favorite competition among robot builders. More than 400 people entered their robots in the Sumo Robot Competition last year in Japan. The rules are exactly the same as for human sumo wrestlers: Push your opponent out of the five-foot-diameter circle within three minutes. Winners receive a million yen, or $7,700 in U.S. currency.

Had enough destruction? Then how about robosport competitions? There's the Hong Kong Robot Ping-Pong Competition, Atomic Hockey, the Walking Machine Decathlon, even robosoccer. Two teams of Korean roboticists went to Brazil in 1997 to help scientists develop machines to compete in the Robo World Cup Initiative. The robots are almost three inches tall and play on a field that is four and a half feet long and three feet wide.

One of the most popular annual robotics competitions is

sponsored by FIRST (For Inspiration and Recognition of Science and Technology), a nonprofit organization whose mission is to interest young people in science and engineering. It was started by Dean Kamen, a New Hampshire–based physicist and inventor, and Dr. Woodie Flowers, professor of Mechanical Engineering at MIT and former host of the PBS series *Scientific American Frontiers.*

FIRST teams up high school students with teachers, university engineering graduate students, and professional engineers. For six weeks they work together designing, building, and testing their robots for the competition, which has different themes and rules each year. In 1997 more than 150 schools, companies, and universities worked together to build "robo-gladiators." Each robot was assembled from identical kits, which included drill motors, batteries, radio remote controllers, pumps, air cylinders, joysticks, modems, and programmable control systems. The teams put the finishing touches on their warriors and then let them go head to head in 120-second elimination rounds.

There are also contests where robots with more civilized qualities can win the day, such as the charming and witty *Coyote,* your host with the most. Coyote was created by a team from the Naval Research Laboratory to compete in

Coyote

the AAAI (American Association for Artificial Intelligence) 1997 Mobile Robot Hors d'Oeuvres Event and is a Nomad 200 mobile robot with an onboard Pentium processor.

Thanks to Coyote's sonar and infrared range sensors, the robot can detect and avoid collisions—a very important feature since the robot made its first appearance mingling with the crowds at the conference reception.

When Coyote does detect an obstacle, it uses an infrared motion detector to determine whether the obstacle is a person. If so, Coyote then graciously offers the person an hors d'oeuvre (no fish eggs or fondue, just peanuts and pretzels). Another motion detector tells Coyote when an hors d'oeuvre has been taken so it can respond with the question, "Are you sure you're making the right decision?" (The question is a quote from HAL, the superbrainy computer from the movie *2001: A*

Coyote serving cocktails

Space Odyssey.) In addition, Coyote remembers the locations where it has offered hors d'oeuvres so it can move on to new people.

But what really clinched the first-place technical award and second-place People's Choice award were Coyote's jokes: the robot keeps up a flow of one-liners as it moves along.

There are resources on the Web for robot hobbyists, clubs, competitions, equipment, and toys. One of the best sites to find everything you need (including more about all the robots and robot-related topics in this book) is *www.robotics.com/robots.html.*

And in case you're wondering, BioHazard whipped La Machine's mechanical rear end at Robot Wars in about eighteen seconds. La Machine put up a good fight but was ultimately unable to get underneath BioHazard's skirt of armor. La Machine was flipped upside down and lost.

BioHazard's creator, Carlo Bertocchini, also built a robot named The Beast, which won the Sumo Robot Competition, and he was captain of the joint Raychem Corp./Woodside High School team that built Stealth, which won the FIRST competition.

Why does Carlo want to build a great robot like Bio-Hazard and then watch it get pounded?

"The challenge is to build a better robot than everybody else," he says. "When you get into the arena to do battle, each of the decisions that you made along the way will be tested. If you win, then you have the satisfaction of knowing that those decisions were better than those made by your opponent."

Oh, and one more thing Carlo neglected to mention . . . it's terrific fun!

How to Build Your Own Robot

If you are interested in building your own robot, you might want to visit the following Web sites:

KrisTech Robot Magazine
www.robotmag.com

Robotix
www.learningtoys.com

Solarbotics
www.solarbotics.com

TechKids
www.hompro.com/techkids

Mondo-tronics' Robot Store
www.robotstore.com/index.html

Glossary

Aaron: A robot programmed to create original artwork, developed by artist Harold Cohen.

AER Camera: The acronym for Autonomous Extravehicular Robotic Camera. A free-flying camera for use in association with the space shuttle and space station; developed by the NASA Telerobotics Program.

AESOP 3000: A voice-controlled robot capable of moving and positioning an endoscope, which is a probe with a tiny camera attached.

Algorithm: A process for defining the steps necessary in order to carry out a specific task.

Andros Mark V: A mobile robot used for hazardous duty that can maneuver over rough terrain and also climb stairs; developed by Remotec, Inc.

Andros VI-A: A smaller version of the Mark V.

Andros 6X6: The largest, strongest mobile robot used for hazardous duty; developed by Remotec, Inc.

Antbot: A tiny robot modeled on ants that behaves cooperatively for the greater good of the group; developed by James McLurkin at MIT.

Artificial Intelligence: Programming something inanimate, such as a machine, with intelligence.

BioHazard: A 4.5-inch-high steel robot.

Bottom-Up System: A system of robotic intelligence that starts at the bottom, or "feet," of the machine and works up; developed by Rodney Brooks at MIT.

Chatterbot: A verbally enhanced, artificially intelligent entity.

Cog: A robot programmed to have five senses, like humans; developed by Rodney Brooks.

Coyote: A robot that serves hors d'oeuvres; created by a team from the Naval Research Laboratory.

Cyc: A robot programmed with the knowledge of an encyclopedia; developed by Doug Lenat.

Dante: An upright-walking robot that explored the volcano Mount Erebus; developed by the Carnegie-Mellon Robotics Center.

Dante II: An upright-walking robot that explored and took samples of the Mount Spurr volcano; developed by the Carnegie-Mellon Robotics Center.

Deep Blue: A chess-playing supercomputer developed by scientists at IBM.

Echolocation: A sensory process in certain animals in which high-pitched sounds are made and their echoes interpreted to determine the direction and distance of objects.

Genghis: The first walking insect robot, developed by Rodney Brooks at MIT's Mobot Laboratory.

Hazardous Duty: A job that is life threatening, such as fire fighting, mine detection, or bomb detonation.

Infrared: Invisible wavelengths that are shorter than radio waves.

Julia: A verbally enhanced, artificially intelligent entity (a chatterbot); developed by Michael Mauldin at Carnegie-Mellon.

Julie: A verbally enhanced computer program; developed by Richard Gibbons of Vancouver Island, B.C.

Ka: A verbally enhanced, artificially intelligent entity.

La Machine: A robot created by La Ma Motors for Robot Wars.

Long-Reach Manipulator: A robotic device used to reach something in the distance.

Mars Pathfinder: The spacecraft used to carry the robot Sojourner to Mars.

Microrobots: Robots built on a microscopic scale.

Micro-rover: A very small rover developed by NASA for planetary exploration.

Mini-Andros: A mobile robot used for hazardous duty developed by Remotec, Inc.

Nanorobots: Robots built on a microscopic scale.

Nanotechnology: Technology on a microscopic scale.

NASA: The acronym for the National Aeronautics and Space Administration.

Nomad: An upright-walking, remote-controlled robot developed as a joint project between Carnegie-Mellon and NASA Ames Research Center to explore and collect rock samples from another planet.

One-Legged Hopper: A robot that hops on one "leg" like a pogo stick. Developed by Marc Raibert at the Leg Lab at MIT.

Precursor: One that comes before another; a predecessor.

RMI: The acronym for Remote Mobile Investigator. A remote-controlled robot owned by the Baltimore City Fire Department.

Robo-kitten: A robot whose actions and behavior are modeled on those of a kitten; developed by Dr. Hugo de Garis at Tokyo University.

Robo-roach: A cockroach with a surgically implanted microprocessor and electric backpack; developed at Tokyo University.

Robot III: A robot modeled on a cockroach; developed at Case Western Reserve University.

Robotic Arm: An instrument that can help doctors perform surgical procedures.

Robotic Probe: An instrument used in brain surgery.

Robotic Room: A room equipped with sensors that enable it to "watch" a patient.

Robotics: The science or study of the technology associated with the design, fabrication, and application of robots.

Robot Wars: A robot competition where robots go head-to-head in a contest of strength, power, and intelligence.

Rockettes: Ten-gram mobile microrobots used for planetary exploration; developed at the MIT Artificial Intelligence Laboratory.

Rocky 7: A robot being developed by NASA for intensive Mars exploration.

Rodolph: A robot modeled on a dolphin. Like a dolphin, Rodolph uses echolocation to recognize objects; developed by Roman Luc at Yale University.

Rover: A robot sheepdog; created by Richard Vaughn at the University of Oxford in England.

Serial Processing: A system in which information is transmitted piece by piece to a computer chip, which in turn relays instructions step by step.

Sojourner: The first Mars rover robot, launched in December 1996; developed by NASA's Jet Propulsion Laboratory.

Spring Flamingo: A walking robot developed by Jerry Pratt at MIT's Leg Laboratory.

STAR: The acronym for Spiral Track Autonomous Robot. STAR detects land mines; developed by the Lawrence Livermore Laboratory.

Sylvie: A verbally enhanced, artificially intelligent entity; created by Michael Mauldin at Carnegie-Mellon.

Teleport: To experience a space event via remote control and virtual reality.

Telepresence: A presence established via remote control and virtual reality.

Telesurgery: Surgery via remote control.

Toddler: A robot that learns the way a young child (or toddler) learns; developed by Tom Miller at the University of New Hampshire.

Top-Down System: A system of robotic intelligence that starts at the top, or "head," of the machine and works down.

Transducer: A substance or device that converts one form of energy into another.

Verbot: A verbally enhanced, artificially intelligent entity.

Virtual Mode Control: A system by which a robot is given artificial balance.

Virtual Reality: A computer-generated environment in which people can interact.

Wanda: Modeled on a pike fish, this robot was created to study how fish swim; developed by John Muir Kamph at MIT's Department of Ocean Engineering.

Bibliography

"Battle of the Robots." *National Geographic World* (August 1998), pp. 24–27.

Blackburn, Carol. "Exploring Career Options: Robotics; Interview with Greg Chirikjian." *Imagine* (a publication of the Johns Hopkins Institute for the Academic Advancement of Youth) vol. 5 no. 3 (January/February 1998), pp. 18–20.

Boden, Margaret A. "Artificial Genius." *Discover* (October 1996), pp. 105–113.

Hendricks, Melissa. "At the Slithering Frontier of Robotics." *Johns Hopkins Magazine* vol. XLVI, no. 2 (April 1994), pp. 48–51.

Quittner, Joshua. "What's Hot in Bots." *Time* (December 8, 1997), p. 31.

Wickelgren, Ingrid. *Ramblin' Robots: Building a Breed of Mechanical Beasts.* New York: Franklin Watts, 1996.

Index

Page numbers in *italics* refer to illustrations.